D0767245

IMAGINE THAT™

Licensed exclusively to Imagine That Publishing Ltd
Tide Mill Way, Woodbridge, Suffolk, IP12 1AP, UK
www.imaginethat.com
Copyright © 2019 Imagine That Group Ltd
All rights reserved
2 4 6 8 9 7 5 3
Manufactured in China

Written by Oakley Graham
Illustrated by Gareth Llewhellin

All rights reserved. No part of this publication may be reproduced, stored in a retrieval system, or transmitted in any form or by any means, electronic, mechanical, photocopying, recording or otherwise, without the prior written permission of the publisher. Neither this book nor any part or any of the illustrations, photographs or reproductions contained in it shall be sold or disposed of otherwise than as a complete book, and any unauthorised sale of such part illustration, photograph or reproduction shall be deemed to be a breach of the publisher's copyright.

ISBN 978-1-78958-268-0

A catalogue record for this book is available from the British Library

Goodnight, I Love You

Written by Oakley Graham

Illustrated by Gareth Llewhellin

I love you. You are safe.
It's time to find a happy place.

Close your eyes and come with me,
We're going on a dream journey.

I love you. You are safe.
It's time to find a happy place.

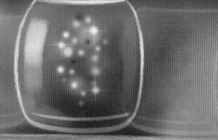
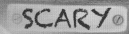

SCARY

HAPPY

SAD

Put your worries on the shelf.
You can do it all by yourself.

I love you. You are safe.
It's time to find a happy place.

Stretch out your legs and then each arm,
I will always keep you safe from harm.

I love you. You are safe.
It's time to find a happy place.

Now picture this … here comes a train,
To take away bad thoughts and pain.

I love you. You are safe.
It's time to find a happy place.

Breathe in deeply, count to three,
You're walking by the sparkling sea.

I love you. You are safe.
It's time to find a happy place.

It's sunny and you're at the park.
Climbing trees with bumpy bark.

I love you. You are safe.
It's time to find a happy place.

Ice cream on a summer's day.
Friends invite you out to play!

I love you. You are safe.
It's time to find a happy place.

Let's rise up towards the stars,
To float and play for hours and hours.

I love you. You are safe.
It's time to find a happy place.

Now we're in the sea so deep,
What will you spy, before you sleep?

I love you. You are safe.
It's time to find a happy place.

Run in the woods, free as can be,
Side by side, just you and me.

I love you. You are safe.
It's time to find a happy place.

It's getting late, time for bed,
Now rest your little sleepy head.

Goodnight. I love you.